Friday Night Is Papa Night

FRIDAY NIGHT IS PAPA NIGHT

Ruth A. Sonneborn
Illustrated by Emily A. McCully

Puffin Books

PUFFIN BOOKS
A Division of Penguin Books USA Inc.
375 Hudson Street, New York, New York 10014
Penguin Books Ltd, Harmondsworth, Middlesex, England
Penguin Books Australia Ltd, Ringwood, Victoria, Australia
Penguin Books Canada Limited, 10 Alcorn Avenue, Toronto, Ontario, Canada M4V 3B2
Penguin Books (N.Z.) Ltd, 182–190 Wairau Road, Auckland 10, New Zealand

First published by The Viking Press, 1970
Published in Picture Puffins 1987
9 10
Text copyright © Ruth A. Sonneborn, 1970
Illustrations copyright © Emily A. McCully, 1970
All rights reserved
Printed in the United States of America
Set in Melior Bold

Library of Congress catalog card number: 86-43214
(CIP data available)
ISBN 0-14-050754-X

For Alexis and Alison,
because they asked
to have their names
in a book

Pedro sat on the kitchen floor, pushing two little cars around and around the legs of his bed.

"Is tonight Friday night, Mama?" he asked.

"Yes," Mama said. "Tonight is Friday night."

Pedro clapped his hands. "Papa is coming. Papa is coming," he sang. "Papa comes every Friday, doesn't he, Mama?"

Mama nodded her head. "Now, Pedro," she said. "Get up on your bed. I have to wash the kitchen floor. Stay up there till the floor is dry."

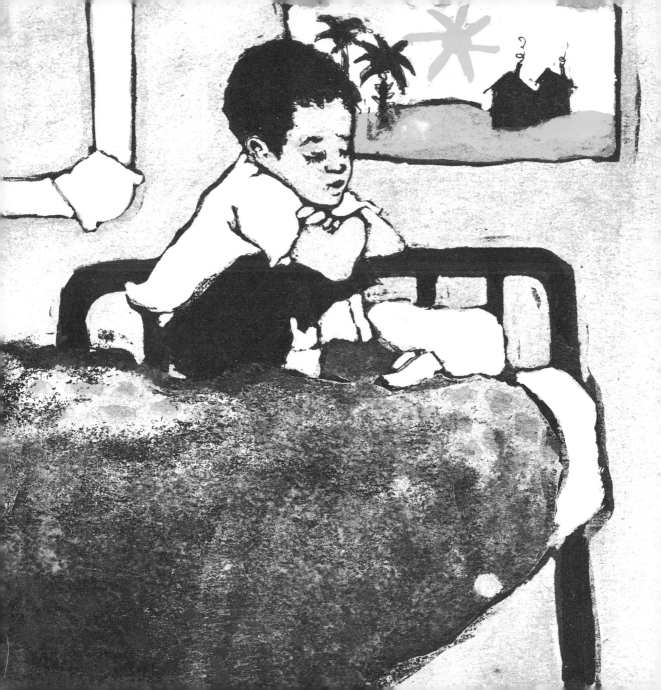

Pedro watched Mama fill the pail with water. He watched the mop slide back and forth across the kitchen floor. It made the floor look so shiny. He was glad his bed was in the kitchen where he could watch Mama work.

"Mama," he said, "why doesn't Papa come home every night? Ana's papa comes home every night. Why not my papa?"

Mama sighed. "Poor Papa," she said, "has to work very hard. He has to have two jobs to get enough money so we can eat and have a place to live. His jobs are far from here, too. Poor, poor Papa. He works so hard for us."

"When I get big," Pedro said, "I'll help Papa. I'll take one of his jobs. Then Papa can come home every night."

"Yes," Mama said. "Some day Papa will come home every night. It will happen, Pedro. It will happen."

The door opened, and Manuela, Carlos, and Ricardo came in together from school.

"Tonight is Friday night," Pedro shouted. "Papa is coming."

"Who doesn't know that, silly?" Carlos said.

"Never mind the talk," Mama said. "We have work to do. Everyone gets a job.

"You, Manuela, you wash and pick over the beans." Mama pointed to the sink.

"You, Carlos, run to the store. I forgot to buy onions." She handed Carlos her purse.

"And you, Ricardo, take the trash downstairs, please, and dump it."

"What about me?" Pedro asked. "Don't I get a job?"

"Sure," Mama said. "You get a job, too. Here, help your brother. Take this small basket of trash down."

By late afternoon the jobs were done. The table was set. The kitchen was filled with smells that made everyone hungry.

Pedro went to the window. He stared down into the street. It was beginning to grow dark.

"I don't see Papa," he said.

Manuela looked at the kitchen clock. "He's awfully late already, Mama," she said. "What could have happened?"

"Don't worry," Mama said. "Papa will come."

"Yes," Pedro said. "Papa always comes on Friday." He pressed his face against the windowpane. "Look," he said. "The street lights are on now. Where is Papa?"

They waited and waited.

Finally, Mama went to the stove.

"Come, niños," she said. "We must eat. Papa will come while we eat."

The children came to the table. No one talked.

Then Pedro said, "I don't want any supper. I want Papa." He began to cry.

Manuela patted him. She wiped his eyes and helped him blow his nose. Pedro got up from the table and crawled onto his bed. He put his head on his pillow. Mama came over. She covered him with a blanket.

"O.K., Pedro," she said. "Go to sleep now."

Pedro sat up. "No, no, no," he shouted. "I don't want to sleep. I want to wait for Papa."

Mama hugged him. "Go to sleep now, Pedro," she said. "I will wake you when Papa comes."

"Sure?" Pedro asked. "Promise?"

"Promise," Mama said.

Pedro's eyes closed.

Suddenly Pedro awoke. He opened his eyes. The kitchen was very dark and empty. There was just one spot of light on the floor by the window.

Pedro sat up in bed.

And then he remembered.

Papa. Papa had not come home.

There on the kitchen table was Papa's plate, his fork, his knife, his spoon, his glass, his napkin—still on the table. All clean and unused.

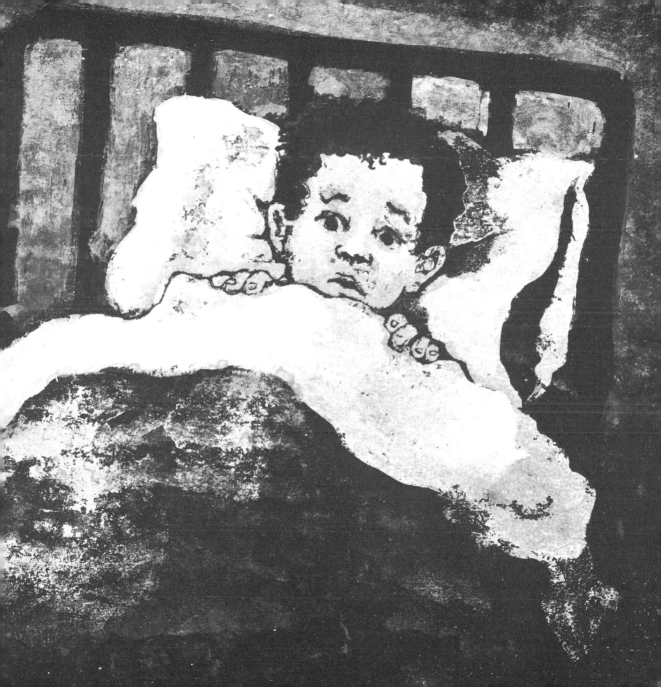

Pedro got out of bed and ran to the window. He looked down into the street. A noisy car drove by. Two people walked past.

Where was Papa? Why hadn't he come home?

Pedro pulled a chair over to the window. He knelt on it and stared into the street. There was no one there. Then a cat ran across the street. A policeman walked slowly past.

He saw a dark shadow moving. The shadow moved closer. Was it? Yes, it was a man. It was a man carrying a fat shopping bag. Papa always brought a fat shopping bag home with him. The man came closer. Papa! Pedro was sure it was Papa.

He hurried across the kitchen and turned on the light. The kitchen now looked brighter than day.

He ran to the door and opened it wide.

"Papa," Pedro shouted. "Papa, you're here."

He hugged Papa and Papa hugged him.

In another minute Mama, Manuela, Ricardo, and Carlos came running from their beds.

"Papa, Papa, what happened?" everyone asked at the same time.

"What happened?" Papa said. "I'll tell you what happened. My friend Juan who works with me got sick. I took him to the hospital. Then I went to tell his wife. I couldn't get home sooner. You understand, niños?"

"We should have a phone," Carlos said. "Everyone else has a phone."

"I know, but a phone costs money," Mama said. She took Papa by the hand. "Come, sit down. You must be very tired."

Papa sat down. "You know," he said, "coming home now I was so tired. So very tired. I looked up at the window. It was dark. I thought, now I have to climb the stairs. Now I have to go into a dark apartment. Everyone will be sleeping. No one will be at the door to meet me. But suddenly there was a light in the kitchen window. Someone was up. Someone was waiting. And"—he pulled Pedro onto his lap—"it was my Pedro. My Pedro had turned on the light. My Pedro was at the door waiting for me. And suddenly I was not tired any more."

Papa hugged Pedro and set him down on the floor. He drew the fat shopping bag toward him.

"Come now," he said. "Let's begin." He dipped his hand into the bag.

"Popsicles," the children shouted. Papa always brought Popsicles.

"Popsicles in the middle of the night?" Mama said. "Whoever heard of Popsicles in the middle of the night?"

Papa dug again into the shopping bag.

He handed out . . .
sneakers for Pedro
a blouse for Manuela
socks for Carlos
pajamas for Ricardo

and to Mama he gave one red rose.

"It's just like Christmas when Papa comes home," Pedro said. "Just like Christmas."

Mama heaped Papa's plate with fish and beans and everyone sat around the table talking, laughing, watching Papa eat.

"Yes," Pedro said dreamily, "Friday night is the nicest night. Friday night is Papa night."